Being HME

written by
Traci Sorell

illustrated by
Michaela Goade

Kokila

Here,

cars rush,

crowds collect.

Etsi says this is not our rhythm.

More houses go up.

Fewer animal relatives visit.

Our family is too far away.

But soon it'll be different because . . .

Today is moving day!

"See you later, house."

"Gotta go, swing."

Time to head home
and change our *tempo*.

Etsi says we're on a new path.
One that leads us to
our ancestors' land
and to our people.
I'm ready.

Singing,
shell shaking,
storytelling,
stickball playing
all offer different beats.

Time to unload.

Pick up the pace.

Everyone's here to help.

Done!

Now to *explore.*

"*Siyo*, animal relatives."

"You look great, swing."

Let's play!

No more busy streets.
Room to run, ride, or roll along.

No more crowded spaces.
I hear the creek, cool and constant.

No more faraway family.
Close enough to gather, eat,
laugh, dance, and share.

I love the rhythm of being home.

For Carlos and his elisi (my etsi), who led us back home
—T. S.

For the dreamers and the doodlers
—M. G.

Glossary

Etsi (eh-gee): Mother
Siyo (see-yo): Hi
Elisi (eh-lee-see): Grandmother

KOKILA
An imprint of Penguin Random House LLC, New York

First published in the United States of America by Kokila, an imprint of Penguin Random House LLC, 2024

Text copyright © 2024 by Traci Sorell
Illustrations copyright © 2024 by Michaela Goade

Visit us online at PenguinRandomHouse.com.

Library of Congress Cataloging-in-Publication Data is available.

ISBN 9781984816030

1 3 5 7 9 10 8 6 4 2

Manufactured in China
TOPL

This book was edited by Namrata Tripathi and designed by Jasmin Rubero.
The production was supervised by Tabitha Dulla, Nicole Kiser, Ariela Rudy Zaltzman, and Caitlin Taylor.

Text set in Diverda Serif Com.

The art for this book was created with watercolor,
colored pencils, pencil, gouache, and digital techniques.